A Hat for
MINERVA
LOUISE

Janet Morgan Stoeke

PUFFIN BOOKS

■

For Colin Wilcox Brooks

■

PUFFIN BOOKS
Published by the Penguin Group
Penguin Books USA Inc., 375 Hudson Street, New York, New York 10014, U.S.A.
Penguin Books Ltd, 27 Wrights Lane, London W8 5TZ, England
Penguin Books Australia Ltd, Ringwood, Victoria, Australia
Penguin Books Canada Ltd, 10 Alcorn Avenue, Toronto, Ontario, Canada M4V 3B2
Penguin Books (N.Z.) Ltd, 182-190 Wairau Road, Auckland 10, New Zealand
Penguin Books Ltd, Registered Offices: Harmondsworth, Middlesex, England

First published in the United States of America by Dutton Children's Books,
a division of Penguin Books USA Inc., 1994
Published in Puffin Books, 1997

1 3 5 7 9 10 8 6 4 2

THE LIBRARY OF CONGRESS HAS CATALOGED THE DUTTON EDITION AS FOLLOWS:
Stoeke, Janet Morgan.
A hat for Minerva Louise / by Janet Morgan Stoeke.—1st ed.
p.   cm.
Summary: Minerva Louise, a snow-loving chicken,
mistakes a pair of mittens for two hats to keep both ends warm.
ISBN 0-525-45328-8
[1. Chickens—Fiction. 2. Hats—Fiction.] I. Title.
PZ7.S8696Hat   1994   [E] — dc20   94-2139   CIP   AC

Puffin Books ISBN 0-14-055666-4
Printed in the U.S.A.

Minerva Louise loved snowy mornings.

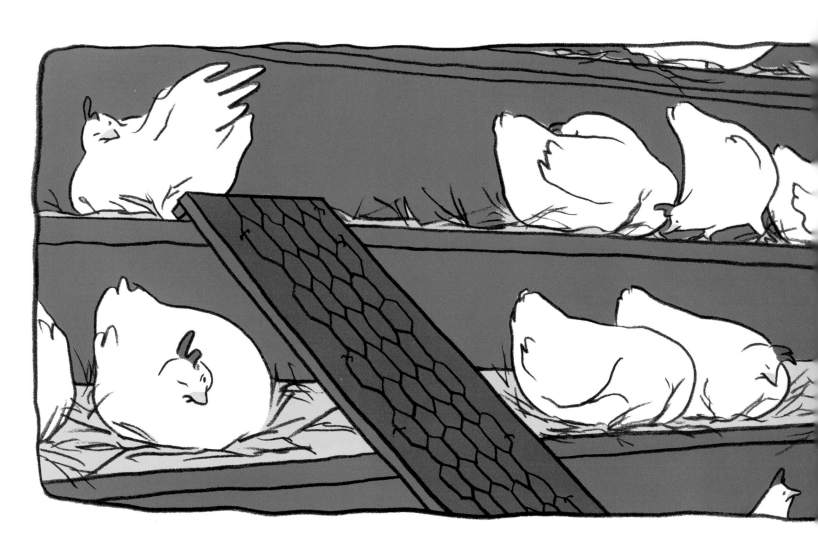

Her friends didn't like them one bit.

They stayed inside all day with their heads tucked under their wings.

Not Minerva Louise. She couldn't
wait to go out exploring.

Everything was so beautiful!

She wanted to stay out all day.
But it was too cold.

If I had some warm things like you,
she said, I could stay out and play.

A scarf might help.

But not this one. It's way too big.

And these shoes are too big, too.

A hat! That's just what I need.

But not this one.

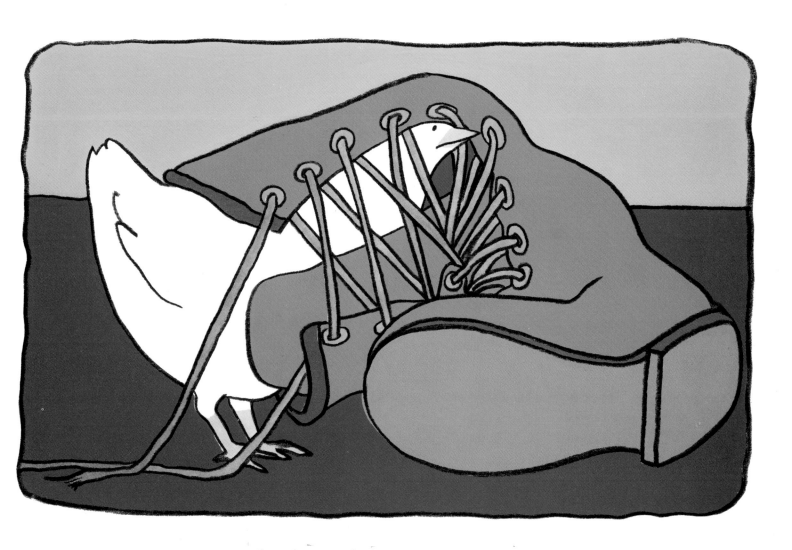

And not this one, either.
It's too heavy.

There must be a hat around
here somewhere.

Minerva Louise looked outside.
Everyone had on a fluffy white hat!

Oh, *your* hat is wonderful!
Where did you get it?

Oh, look! What's over here?

A hat! It's perfect. But what's this?

Oh, it's two hats!

Which was just fine

with Minerva Louise.